The Clean-Up of Codfish Cove

Published by

Third Story Books™
955 Connecticut Avenue, Suite 1302
Bridgeport, Connecticut 06607

ISBN 1-884506-05-4

Distributed to the trade by
Andrews & McMeel
4900 Main Street
Kansas City, Missouri 64112

Library of Congress Catalog Card Number: 93-61824

Printed in Singapore

The Clean-Up

of CODFISH COVE

A book about the environment by GARY A. LEWIS

Illustrated by WILLIAM LANGLEY STUDIOS

THIRD™
STORY
BOOKS

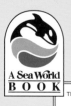

A Sea World
BOOK™

Dear Grown-up:

When SEA WORLD opened its doors in 1964, it had a mission. That mission was to give adults and children a chance to see and learn about all the creatures of the sea . . . and to help preserve these creatures for future generations.

SEA WORLD books have a similar mission. They were created to entertain, and to help teach children something about the wonderful creatures that call the oceans home. And all books in this series are approved by the Education Department at SEA WORLD.

But SEA WORLD books teach kids other things, too—such as the importance of friendship, of self-esteem, of caring for our planet and for one another. Most importantly, SEA WORLD books accomplish their "missions" by telling stories about the wonderful creatures of the sea— stories your children will love to experience again and again.

By the way, when you've finished reading the story in this SEA WORLD book, don't forget to take a look at the two pages that follow the story. On them are some seaworthy facts about things in the story that you and your children might find interesting.

Welcome to SEA WORLD books. We hope your whole family enjoys them . . . and learns a little something from them, too!

Sincerely,
The Publishers

Shamu loved the ocean around Codfish Cove. He loved the sea when it was warm and gentle and lapped at the shore. He loved it when it was cold and gray. He loved to leap high out of the water and land on his side. He loved to swim circles around and around in the cove.

He even loved it when it stormed, when the wind was blowing, Sir Winston's rowboat was tossed to and fro, and giant waves crashed against his big, sleek body as he swam.

Codfish Cove was home.

But one day, Shamu saw something in Codfish Cove that made him frown. It was a large, black thing that floated on the water like a giant stain.

Baby Shamu thought it was a toy. He poked his nose into it and dove deep, dragging it behind him.

But Shamu knew it was not a toy. It was trash. And it was an ugly thing that did not belong in his ocean.

Over the next few weeks, Shamu began to notice more trash floating in the waters of Codfish Cove. There were bottles and cans, paper and plastic. The sight filled Shamu's heart with sadness.

So Shamu called a meeting of his friends. They all gathered in Codfish Cove.

"It is time to leave this place," Shamu said. "We must go to where the waters are clean and it is safe for us to swim and play."

Sir Winston Walrus frowned. "Shamu," he said, "in my younger days, I was captain of a ship that traveled the seven seas. You will have to go far, far away to find such a place."

"Then I will go there," Shamu said simply.

Later, Sir Winston sat in his cabin with O.P. Otter, Virgil Pelican and
Seamore and Clyde Sea Lion.

"I don't want to leave," said O.P. "And neither does Clancy Clam. We
love it here in Codfish Cove."

"We do, too," added Seamore.

"I cannot go," Sir Winston said. "I am far too old to find a new home."

"What can we do?" Clyde asked.

Sir Winston got up. He paced back and forth while the others watched.
Finally he sat down again with a sigh. "I don't know," he admitted.

Just then, Virgil Pelican whispered something into O.P.'s ear. "Sir
Winston," O.P. said. "Virgil has an idea."

"Well, what is it? Speak up, sailor," Sir Winston rumbled.

"Virgil says we have to get rid of all the stuff that's floating in Codfish Cove," said O.P. "If we clean it up, maybe Shamu won't go away. And we won't have to go, either."

Sir Winston thought for a long time. Then he began to smile. "I see it now!" he said. "We must clean up Codfish Cove. We must make it shipshape again, so that Shamu will want to stay."

The very next day, the clean-up of Codfish Cove began.
"But we won't tell Shamu," Dolly suggested. "We'll surprise him."

Everyone who lived in Codfish Cove worked very hard all that day and into the night. They wanted the ocean to be spotless and beautiful once more. They loved their home, and they wanted to stay. Most of all, they wanted Shamu to stay.

When all the garbage was gathered on the beach, Clyde and O.P. separated it into neat piles. Sir Winston called for a garbage pickup from his cabin.

The next morning was clear and bright. Sir Winston stood at his window, looking out at the sea.

The waters sparkled in the sun. They were clean and beautiful again.

Later that day, Sir Winston and the others went out to visit Shamu.

"What has happened to all the garbage?" Shamu asked. "Where has it gone?"

"We cleaned it up, Shamu," O.P. said happily. "We worked all day and night. We want to stay in Codfish Cove. And we want you to stay, too."

Just then, Virgil noticed something. "Milk carton off the port stern, Captain!" he squawked.

"Oh, no," Sir Winston said. "There's more." He bowed his head sadly. "And there will be more, and more, and more. I see it now, Shamu. We were wrong. Perhaps you and the others must leave after all."

Shamu looked at his old friend. Then he shook his giant head.

"No, Sir Winston," he said. "*I* was wrong. We cannot run away from our problems. We must stay and solve them. If we do not clean up Codfish Cove, soon the garbage here will float to other places. And someday, *all* the waters of the ocean will be full of garbage . . . and there will be nowhere we can go to escape it."

Shamu gently picked up the carton in his mouth and dropped it into the bottom of Sir Winston's boat.

And so Shamu and his Crew stayed in Codfish Cove. And from that day on, the clean-up of Codfish Cove took place every morning, rain or shine.

"For, as Shamu says," Sir Winston was fond of repeating, "if *we* do not keep our home clean, who will?"

Ahoy, There!

This is Shamu...and here
are some seaworthy facts for you!

What Is Pollution?

When garbage and waste products clutter up the world we live in, that's *pollution.* Garbage is all the stuff we throw away—old tissues, rubber tires, bottles and cans, and tons of other things. Waste products can come from the things we make or do. Burning coal to make heat, for instance, also makes smoke and different gases as waste products. All these things . . . and lots more . . . can pollute our world.

In THE CLEAN-UP OF CODFISH COVE, Shamu's friends all join together to clean up Codfish Cove. But in real life, the fish and mammals of the ocean can't clean their homes themselves. We have to do it for them. And just like Shamu and his crew, we can't run away from pollution. If we do, it will just get worse and worse. Soon, it will follow us around until all the world's seas—and the land around them—are full of garbage.

What Can You Do About Pollution?

Here are a couple of things you can do to make the seas—and the land—better for everyone!

1 **String Along.** Never let a balloon float away from you. Balloons look pretty flying up in the sky. But they can drift out over the ocean . . . and that means trouble for sea creatures. When the balloons lose their air or helium and land in the water, they are sometimes eaten by fish and sea mammals. This can make these creatures very sick . . . and even kill them. So hold onto those strings!

2 **Water, water everywhere?** Water is very precious. Without it, the creatures of the sea wouldn't survive . . . and neither would you! So don't waste it. Don't run water while you're brushing your teeth; fill your glass instead. Also, when you're thirsty, don't let water run until it's cold; keep some cold water in a jar in the refrigerator.

3 **At the Beach.** One thing you can do to help keep beaches clean is to bring along a garbage bag every time you go. Whenever you see litter on the beach, put it in the bag and bring it home for disposal or recycling. You might also want to know that the third Saturday in September is International Coastal Clean-Up Day. Call the Center for Marine Conservation in Washington, D.C. for information.

4 **Remember: recycle!** Lots of garbage can be used to make new stuff. For instance, old bottles, cans, and newspapers can be used to make new bottles, cans, and newspapers. Recycling saves energy. This means we need to send less oil from place to place . . . And that means there's less of a chance for an oil barge to have an accident and spill oil into the ocean.

These days, most towns and cities have recycling programs. Find out what is recycling in your neighborhood. Then make sure to gather these things up so that they can be collected for recycling. Shamu will thank you for it!

Sea World®

"For in the end we will conserve only what we love.
We will love only what we understand.
And we will understand only what we are taught."

Baba Dioum — noted Central African Naturalist

Since the first Sea World opened in 1964, more than 160 million people have experienced first-hand the majesty and mystery of marine life. Sea World parks have been leaders in building public understanding and appreciation for killer whales, dolphins, and a vast variety of other sea creatures.

Through its work in animal rescue and rehabilitation, breeding, animal care, research and education, Sea World demonstrates a strong commitment to the preservation of marine life and the environment.

Sea World provides all its animals with the highest-quality care including state-of-the-art facilities and stimulating positive reinforcement training programs. Each park employs full-time veterinarians, trainers, biologists and other animal care experts to provide 24-hour care. Through close relationships with these animals — relationships that are built on trust — Sea World's animal care experts are able to monitor their health every day to ensure their well-being. In short, all animals residing at Sea World are treated with respect, love and care.

If you would like more information about Sea World books, please write to us. We'd like to hear from you.

THIRD STORY BOOKS
955 Connecticut Avenue, Suite 1302
Bridgeport, CT 06607